Just Because

MATTHEW McCONAUGHEY

illustrated by **Renée Kurilla**

VIKING

Just because they threw the dart,

doesn't mean that it stuck.

Just because I've got skills,

doesn't mean
there is no luck.

Just because they let you down,
doesn't mean you gotta get low.

Just because they're clumsy,
doesn't mean they have no flow.

Just because you answer,

doesn't mean you
heed the call.

Just because I'm at the top,
doesn't mean I cannot fall.

Just because I let go,

doesn't mean that
I stopped climbing.

Just because
I mean it,

doesn't mean that
I'm not lying.

Just because I'm finished,

doesn't mean that
I'm done.

Just because you
got the gold,

doesn't mean that
you won.

Just because you wrote it,
doesn't mean that I read it.

Just because I did it again,
doesn't mean I don't regret it.

Just because you can pull it off,
doesn't mean that you should do it.

Just because you failed,
doesn't mean that you blew it.

Just because they say it's so,

doesn't mean it happened to me.

There's how I see it,

how you see it,

and what will
come to be.

Just because you
threw shade,

doesn't mean I'm
out of the sun.

Just because they
shut me down,

doesn't mean
I have not won.

Just because you're wailing,
doesn't mean that you're a crier.

Just because I lied,
doesn't mean that
I'm a liar.

Just because they can choose,
doesn't mean you have a choice.

Just because they don't hear you,
doesn't mean you have no voice.

Just because it's silent,
doesn't mean that it's not loud.

Just because you're alone,
doesn't mean there's not a crowd.

Just because I'm dirty,
doesn't mean I can't get clean.

Just because you're nice,
doesn't mean you can't get mean.

Just because I'm
going in circles,

doesn't mean that
I'm dizzy.

Just because I'm sitting still,
doesn't mean that I'm not busy.

Just because we're friends,
doesn't mean that you can't burn me.

Just because I'm stubborn,
doesn't mean that you can't turn me.

Just because I forgive you,
doesn't mean that I still trust.

There's what
you do,

there's what
I do,

and yours is not
my must.

Just because it's fiction,

doesn't mean
it can't be true.

Just because you want one more,

doesn't mean that you need two.

Just because you're a bully,
doesn't mean that you're strong.

Just because it felt right then,
doesn't mean it won't feel wrong.

Just because a hand
is clenched,

doesn't mean that
it's a fist.

Just because
I'd rather not,

doesn't mean
I don't take risks.

Just because I'm in the race,
doesn't mean I'm fully ready.

Just because
you're shaking,

doesn't mean that
you're not steady.

Just because you follow,
doesn't mean you're not a leader.

Just because I keep winning,
doesn't mean that I'm a cheater.

Just because we disagree,
doesn't mean that you're not right.

And just because it's dark,
doesn't mean that it's night.

Just because the sun has set,
doesn't mean it will not rise.

Because every day is a gift,
each one a new surprise.

To my kids, your kids, and the kid in all of us.
We're all as young as we're ever gonna be,
so let's just keep learning.
—McConaughey

VIKING
An imprint of Penguin Random House LLC, New York

First published in the United States of America by Viking,
an imprint of Penguin Random House LLC, 2023

Visit us online at PenguinRandomHouse.com.

Library of Congress Cataloging-in-Publication Data is available.

Manufactured in China

ISBN 9780593622032

1   3   5   7   9   10   8   6   4   2

TOPL

Book design by Pamela Notarantonio
Text set in Henriette

The art for this book was created digitally.